I Want My Sledge!

Licensed by The Illuminated Film Company
Based on the LITTLE PRINCESS animation series © The Illuminated Film Company 2008
Made under licence by Andersen Press Ltd., London
'I Want My Sledge!' episode written by Rachel Murrell.
Producer Iain Harvey. Director Edward Foster.
© The Illuminated Film Company/Tony Ross 2007
Design and layout © Andersen Press Ltd, 2007.
Printed and bound in China by Midas Printing Ltd.
10   9   8   7   6   5   4   3   2   1
British Library Cataloguing in Publication Data available.

ISBN 978 1 84270 832 3

This book has been printed on acid-free paper

I Want My Sledge!

Tony Ross

Andersen Press · London

The Little Princess hummed happily as she finished off
her snowman.

"He needs a carrot," she decided. "For his nose."

She began to hunt around, then glanced over to her sledge.

Maybe she'd have a ride on that instead.

"It goes really fast," giggled the
Little Princess. "Once we even…"

The Chef tapped her on the shoulder.
"Une carotte!"

"Thank you," gasped the Little Princess, dazzled by the Chef's
shiny snowsuit.

The Chef's outfit was matched by an even shinier, sporty
 new sledge.

He gently slid the contraption up to the top of the hill and
climbed aboard.

"*Un, deux, trois*...woohoo!"

He flew past so quickly, Scruff's
ears flapped in the breeze.

The Little Princess ran for the castle.
"D-a-a-a-d!" she cried.

"I want a new sledge!"

"But you already have a sledge," said the King, looking up from his book. "I only made it last year."
"It's too slow!" argued the Little Princess.
"It's quite fast enough for you."

The Little Princess frowned crossly.
"I need a new one!"
"You can't have everything you want," replied
the King. "No!"

The Little Princess was furious. As she sat sulking on her old sledge, the Chef whizzed past again and again on his new one. "I want a sledge like that!"

Ker-plop!

She pulled the carrot out of the snowman's face and munched on it angrily. "Why won't Dad buy me one?" The Little Princess took one more look at the snowman, then started to grin.

The Little Princess burst into the dining room,
clutching the snowman's coin.
"I'm going to buy a new sledge with my own money!"
"I'm afraid that's not enough," the King sighed. "What's
wrong with the old sledge? It's so much fun."
The Little Princess didn't care. "A new one would be
faster and shinier!"

The King had finally agreed to help the Little Princess go faster. He'd been busy with his toolkit for ages.

"Hurry up, Dad!"

At last, he stepped back to reveal… the same old sledge.

"I've polished the skis!" said the King proudly. "And look,
I gave it a bell!"

The Little Princess wasn't impressed.

The King tried not to notice. "Let's go and test it."

The Little Princess and the King climbed aboard.
"See?" chuckled the King. "It's perfectly good."
The sledge trundled slowly down the slope, then gently
zigzagged through the trees. As it came to a halt, a blue
blur shot past them.

It was the Chef on his shiny new sledge!
The King gulped. "All right. You can have a new one."

"Whoopee!" shrieked the Little Princess.

"Come and see what I've got!" the Little Princess called out a few hours later.

Scruff woofed in admiration. The sledge was enormous, shiny and very, very fast. It was also incredibly hard for the Little Princess to push.

"Shall I come too?" beamed the King.
"No, thanks!" cried the Little Princess.
"I want to do it by myself!"

It took a long time for the Little Princess to heave the new sledge up the hill.

At the top she threw teddy Gilbert inside, then used her crown as a step to push herself in.

She stood up to take a deep breath.
"Here...we...go!"

At the bottom of the slope, the Admiral peered through his telescope and gasped.

"Aah! Enemy attack!"

"Look out!" screamed the Little Princess. She ducked down, but the sledge kept going faster and faster and faster.

Cr-a-ss-hhh!

The Little Princess crawled out of the sledge, then
rubbed the snow off.

"It's not the sledge," said the
Little Princess. "The pond
shouldn't be there."

The Admiral was aghast.

"I'm going to have another go," the Little Princess shouted breezily over her shoulder, as she struggled back up the side of the hill and set off again.

"This is better!" she squealed. "Uh-oh."
This time the sledge careered right through
the compost heap.

She and Gilbert were soon hurtling back down
the hill. Sledging was starting to become very
hard work.

"Time for another go," muttered the Little Princess.

"The snowman!" yelled the Little Princess.
"Nooo!!"

But it was too late.

"Right!" she shouted. "That does it.
I've had it with this new sledge!"

"That looks nice," whispered the Little Princess.

"It's a nice little sledge," nodded the King. "How's the new one?"

The Little Princess explained that she was finding the new sledge difficult to handle.

"Maybe you need to be a bit bigger, poppet?"
"Or maybe I need a sledge that's a bit smaller."
The King patted the old sledge, then handed
the reins to the Little Princess.

The Little Princess fluffed up her cushion, then turned
back to Gilbert. "Are you nice and comfy?"
It was time to relaunch her wonderful old sledge, and the
entire royal household had turned out.

"Whheeeeee!" The Little Princess whooped with excitement as she slid down the slope.

"Look at me, Princess!" giggled the Maid, snowboarding down on a tea tray.

Everyone had found their own way to enjoy the snow. It was stacks of fun…

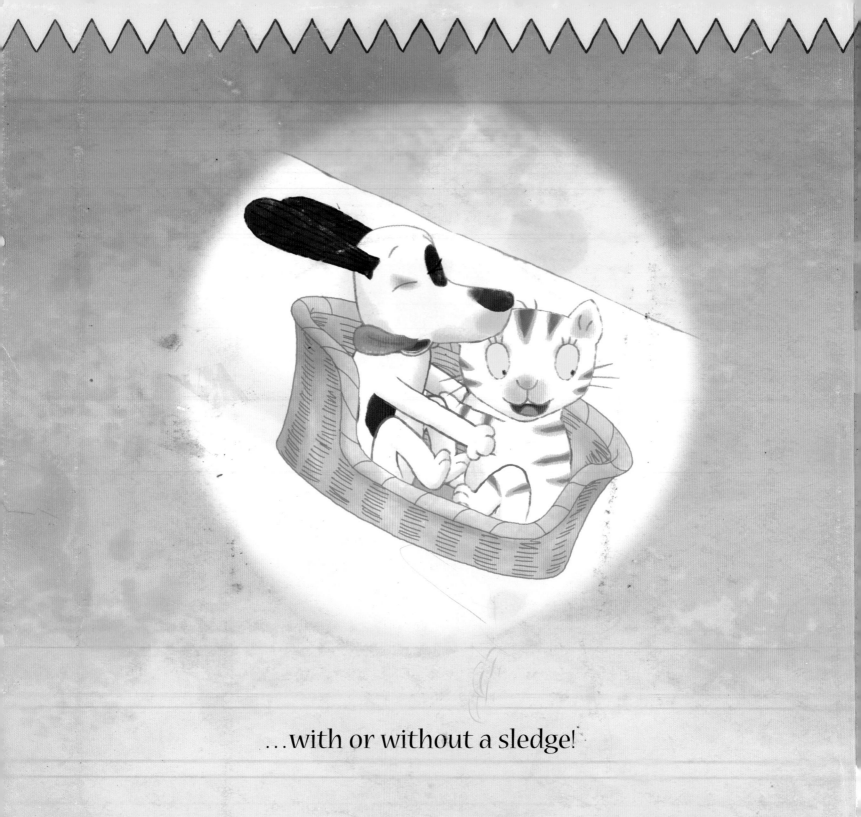

...with or without a sledge!